Chocolate Dirt

By Jacqueline King

iUniverse books may be ordered through booksellers or by contacting:

iUniverse
1663 Liberty Drive
Bloomington, IN 47403
www.iuniverse.com
844-349-9409

Because of the dynamic nature of the Internet, any web addresses or links contained in this book may have changed since publication and may no longer be valid. The views expressed in this work are solely those of the author and do not necessarily reflect the views of the publisher, and the publisher hereby disclaims any responsibility for them.

Any people depicted in stock imagery provided by Getty Images are models, and such images are being used for illustrative purposes only.
Certain stock imagery © Getty Images.

KJV
Scripture taken from The Holy Bible, King James Version. Public Domain

ISBN: 978-1-6632-1970-1 (sc)
ISBN: 978-1-6632-1971-8 (e)

Library of Congress Control Number: 2021905149

Print information available on the last page.

iUniverse rev. date: 04/19/2021

Dedication

This book is dedicated to my Goddaughter Alaya Blair.
The color of your skin does not uphold
who you are as a person, it is just an exterior complexity,
your true beauty is not based on skin
color, it is what is inside your heart.

You are altogether beautiful my darling, there is no flaw in you.
Song of Songs 4:7

To my Cacao seeds

Andrew, Khayla and Brandi

God you are the giver of all that is good. I pray that you will Bless my children with the Fruits of The Spirit. Help them to *love*, be full of *joy, peace*, and *patience*. Help them to be *kind, good, faithful,* and *gentle* when dealing with others. Give them *self-control* to bear the fruit so others can see. Amen.

Galatians 5:22

It was a Friday afternoon, Alaya sat on the curb waiting for her mom to pick her up from school. Her little brother Tatum was climbing on the rocks nearby, her friend Devanay came and sat next to her, She said with excitement, "Alaya I heard you are the spelling bee champion this month, you are so smart, is that the medal?" Alaya leaned in closer to let Devanay see the medal.

Devanay admired the medal looking at it from front to back. "It is so shiny. I heard you won against Sammie, he usually wins, all the time". Alaya responded, "well I am the spelling bee champion, now". Devanay said, "You don't look so happy what's wrong?"

Alaya looked at Devanay, she said, "I don't want to talk about it. Devanay replied, "I heard it had something to do with Sammie". Alaya said, "I don't want to talk about it ok?" Devanay said, "sorry Laya". Alaya said, "it's ok, I'm just worried because my mom is going to be mad, the assistant principal gave me this note to give to her I think it's about what happened with Sammie".

Alaya walked slowly towards the car, she stuffed the envelope in her backpack. Tatum ran to the car as soon as he got inside, he said, "Laya got in trouble today". Alaya yelled," be quiet Tatum, I didn't get in trouble". Shawniece smiled, and asked "what are you talking about Tatum?" Alaya hopped in the car she said, "you know how Tatum is mommy he is always saying something he knows nothing about". Shawniece turned around, she noticed the medal around Alaya's neck with a big smile on her face she asked,

"Oh my Alaya what is that around your neck?" Tatum replied, "I know what it is", Shawniece said, "Tatum let Alaya tell me please, "Oh this? I won the spelling bee; I am the spelling bee champion for the month". Shawniece replied, "Alaya that is so awesome I am so proud of you". Alaya replied, "Thank you, mommy".

"Anything else exciting happen at school today?" Alaya hesitated, she looked at Tatum, then she said. "UUhmm, no that's it". Shawniece asked, "how about you Tatum?" Tatum continued fiddling with his seatbelt, then replied, "I kicked the ball over the fence today when we were playing kick ball". Shawniece replied, "wow, you must have kicked that ball really hard huh?" Tatum replied, "yep"

Once they got home Shawniece said, "go get ready for your bath while I make dinner and don't forget to bring me your backpacks so I can check them". Tatum tossed his backpack on the kitchen floor and ran to his room. Alaya walked quickly to her room she closed the door, she went to sit at her desk trying to figure out what to do about the letter. She heard her mom calling from the living room.

"Alaya I need your backpack please". Alaya replied, "ok, here I come". Alaya took the letter from her backpack she held it in her hands, looking around the room. She heard Tatum open the door, she replied, "you need to knock first Tatum, what do you want?" she hid the letter behind her back, "mom said bring her your backpack." Alaya said, "I heard her". Tatum asked, "what's that behind your back?" Alaya said, "nothing, close my door Tatum". Tatum slammed the door and ran down the hall. Alaya took the letter and put it in her desk drawer, she then took her backpack to her mom.

Shawniece was preparing dinner. Baby Brian was sitting in his infant chair near the kitchen table. Alaya asked, "mommy can I play a game on your phone?" Shawniece replied, "sure go ahead Alaya, take your baby brother with you please while I finish dinner".

Alaya sat on the floor with baby Brian in front of her as she looked for games on the phone. Suddenly, a call came in. Alaya saw that it was from her school, she began to panic she pushed the ignore button on the phone. Shawniece called out from the kitchen, "Alaya who is that calling?" Alaya replied, "oh uhmmm I didn't see the name they hung up". Shawniece replied, "ok, if I get another call answer it please".

Alaya replied, "ok", she put the phone on vibrate and continued playing games.

Dinner was ready, they all gathered at the table. As they were eating Shawniece phone rang again, she looked at it and said, "hmmm why would the school be calling me on a Friday evening?" Alaya looked at her mom then at Tatum. Tatum began to say something, Alaya immediately cut him off and said, "maybe it's just a reminder about a meeting or something". Shawniece pushed ignore and continued eating dinner. Alaya let out a sigh of relief.

After dinner Shawniece had finished clearing the dinner table and washing the dishes. Alaya had just finished taking her bath. Shawniece tapped lightly on the door as she entered the room she asked, "are you ready for story time?" Alaya sat up "yes and I already picked the book".

As she began reading the story. Alaya said, "Mommy I gotta give you something". She climbed over Shawniece reached in her desk drawer and pulled out the letter. She slowly handed the letter to Shawniece. Shawniece looked at the letter, she asked "would this have anything to do with the phone call I received this evening?" Alaya replied, "oh you heard the voicemail?" Shawniece said, "yes I did Alaya". Shawniece began reading the letter, she had a look of surprise on her face as she was reading the letter. She folded the letter placed it back in the envelope. and asked Alaya, "Now would you like to tell me your side of the story?"

Alaya sat up said, "ok let me tell you what happened". Shawniece replied, "ok go ahead I'm listening." Alaya began explaining her side of the story "Ok we were sitting in the cafeteria for lunch and Sammie, you know Sammie the one who always bothering people, he kept calling me names for no reason, I told him to stop, then I just ignored him but he just kept calling me this name and he wouldn't stop, and all the kids in the cafeteria were laughing whenever he said it". I got sooo mad and I threw my milk in his face, I know that wasn't nice mommy, but he wouldn't stop calling me that name".

Shawniece said, "Alaya you know it is not polite for you to throw milk on someone, no matter what you should have told the cafeteria assistant." Alaya replied, "mom she wasn't gonna do anything, she never does". Shawniece replied, "I think you could have handled it differently. Alaya whispered, "I know mommy, but I was so angry, he just kept saying it over and over" Shawniece asked, "What name did he call you Laya to cause you to get so get so upset?" Alaya replied, "It was a name I never heard before and I didn't like it". Shawniece asked, "so what did he call you?" Alaya held her head down, and whispered, "chocolate dirt".

Shawniece had a frown on her face, "what did you say, speak up I did not hear you". Alaya took a deep breath as tears began to roll down her face, "he said you so dark you look like chocolate dirt". Shawniece asked, "did you say, chocolate milk?" "That's not so bad." Alaya said in a louder voice. "No, he called me CHOCOLATE DIRT!"
She began crying louder. Shawniece grabbed a Kleenex from the desk and wiped Alaya's face. Shawniece replied, "I can see you are hurt because of this, let's talk about it, do you know why he called you that Alaya?" Alaya replied, "No, well maybe it was because I won the spelling bee and got the medal, Sammie usually wins every month".

They both sat quietly for a moment. Shawniece said, "sit here I will be right back". She left to go to the kitchen when she returned, she sat in the chair and placed two little chocolate candies on the desk. Alaya asked, "are we eating candy before bedtime?" Shawniece replied, "just for tonight, but that is for later".

first, I want you to think about something." Alaya replied, "what do you want me to think about?" Shawniece said softly, "Now think of your favorite chocolate things and vision them in your head and tell me why you like them". Alaya began thinking "uuhhmmm, well, I like chocolate cake, I like chocolate ice cream cones. "What else?" Shawniece asked, Alaya "I like chocolate chip cookies Oh I like the chocolate cereal you buy; I like to drink hot chocolate when it's cold and rainy". Alaya paused for a moment, "Oh I like the chocolate God mommy buys at the mall".

Alaya asked, "Mommy why are we talking about chocolate stuff?" Shawniece replied, "Well Laya I wanted you to see all the yummy things that are made from chocolate". Alaya replied,"Ohhhh, I see, is it because Sammie called me chocolate?" Shawniece replied, "let me finish". Shawniece said, "now Let's talk about dirt".

CACAO SEED

CHOCOLATE

Alaya said, "dirt, what's so good about dirt mommy?"Shawniece replied, "Well there are a lot of good things you can say about dirt most people see dirt as something bad, someone being dirty, but dirt has many good benefits, it is an important part of our environment it helps plants to grow, you can plant all kinds of seeds in dirt and they will grow into different things." Alaya replied, "Oh, I know mommy the bugs like to live in the dirt too like earth worms, Tatum likes playing with those earthworms." Shawniece smiled, "yes he likes earthworms".

Shawniece asked, "do you know what else grows in dirt?, the cacao seed". Alaya asked, "what is a cacao seed?" Shawniece answered, "The cacao seed is used to make chocolate" Alaya's eyes lit up, "you mean chocolate is made from dirt?" Shawniece chuckled, "Well not really but chocolate is made from the cacao seed which is planted in dirt, then there is a long process to make the chocolate". Alaya sat up with a big smile on her face, "Wow mommy that is so cool".

Shawniece said in a soft voice, "you know Alaya people will say mean things to you, things that make you feel sad or angry, when someone says something mean to you or says something to make you feel bad, you need to turn what they said into something positive, something good". Alaya thought for a minute, "Oh, like when Sammie called me chocolate dirt?" Shawniece replied, "exactly." Alaya replied, "I like that mommy".

Shawniece asked, "So how does that make you feel now?" Alaya replied, "Well I still don't like that he called me chocolate dirt, but now I can see something good about it, thank you mommy" she leaned in to give her a big hug. "You're welcome Laya", Shawniece replied. Alaya looked over at the chocolate candy on the desk, "mommy what about the chocolate candy?"

Shawniece replied, "Oh I almost forgot. She handed Alaya the chocolate candy, "ok now open it." Alaya opened the chocolate candy she was about to put it in her mouth. Shawniece said, "wait Laya not so fast, now close your eyes." Alaya replied, "I have to close my eyes to eat chocolate?", Shawniece laughed, "just close them please". Alaya closed her eyes. Shawniece smiled and said, "Now put the chocolate in your mouth but don't chew it just let it melt in your mouth, and while the chocolate is melting in your mouth I want you to think about all the things we talked about tonight, your favorite chocolate foods, the things that grow in the dirt, the cacao seed that makes chocolate, oh, And Sammie", Alaya opened her eyes, "wait Sammie, why am I thinking about Sammie I'm mad at Sammie, I don't want to think about him".

Shawniece said," just close your eyes please when the chocolate melts away then I want you to open your eyes".

Alaya nodded her head from side to side smiling as she thought about the things she just talked about with her mommy, she had all the visions in her head. Chocolate cake, chocolate ice cream, chocolate chip cookies, chocolate cereal, hot chocolate, the cacao seed then she frowned as she thought about Sammie. She slowly opened her eyes and said, "all done".

Shawniece replied, "great job now how do you feel?" Alaya said softly, "well I feel happy about all the things that are made from chocolate; I am excited to learn that chocolate is made from a seed. I am not too happy about Sammie that he called me chocolate dirt, but now I see chocolate dirt can be something good and yummy". Shawniece replied, "that is right Alaya, I am glad you were able to think of something good about this situation,

sometimes you may not be able to think of something good or positive about a situation, but you must remember to handle your anger or sadness in a positive way". Shawniece asked, "what else could you have done instead of throwing milk on Sammie?" Alaya replied, "well I could have told the cafeteria assistant, or the assistant principal, or even tell Sammie how I felt" Shawniece replied, "Yes, that would have been a wise decision". Alaya replied in an angry voice, "I know mommy, but I was sooo angry".

Alaya asked, "mommy are you upset with me?" Shawniece replied, "no Alaya I am not upset with you, but I am not happy about the choice you made when you threw the milk in Sammie's face". Alaya replied, "Mommy, I apologize, and I will apologize to Sammie" Shawniece leaned over and gave Alaya a big hug, and whispered, "I think that is a good idea, ok you have to go brush your teeth before you go sleep".

Alaya hopped out of bed and skipped to the bathroom to brush her teeth. Shawniece stood next to Alaya as she brushed her teeth, Shawniece reached in the bathroom drawer and took out her eyeliner pencil, she asked, "Alaya, when you look at yourself in the mirror, what do you see?"

Alaya stopped brushing her teeth, she looked at her reflection and replied, "I see me." Shawniece wrote the word beautiful on the mirror. Alaya said, "Oh I get it" She put her tooth brush down, Shawniece handed her the pencil. Alaya began writing words on the mirror, she wrote, pretty, smart, cute, spelling bee champ, best big sister. She covered the mirror with positive words about herself. Shawniece handed out her hand for the pencil.

As she began writing she said, "There is room for one more sentence." She wrote, Song of Songs 4:7. Alaya said, "that's from the Bible, what does it mean mommy?" Shawniece replied, "You are altogether beautiful my darling, there is no flaw in you". Alaya smiled the biggest smile, as she leaned over to give Shawniece a hug. Shawniece secretly wiped a tear from her eye and said, "Ok missy let's go it's getting late." They walked back to the room.

Alaya asked as she climbed into bed, "Mommy are we going to read our good night story?" Shawniece said, "sure Laya, where's the book". Alaya said, "mommy I think you told me the best story ever, the story about Chocolate Dirt" Shawniece smiled, "I didn't think of that, it was a good story". Alaya smiled, "yes it was mommy, thank you, I think we can say our prayers now". Alaya began saying her prayers, she even included Sammie. Shawniece kissed Alaya on the forehead. and whispered, "Good night Alaya. Sweet dreams" Alaya replied, "good night mommy, I think I will dream of chocolate".

Reflection Questions

Don't just read about it, talk about it

Reading is a vital part of a child's educational experience. It is imperative that children understand what they read and are given the opportunity to reflect on it This section encourages children to develop their critical thinking skills.

Asking open ended questions help improve children's comprehension and allows them to explore different interpretations of the story. Here are a few questions that will guide you in the process, you can use these questions or come up with some of your own. There are no right or wrong answers to these questions. The answers are the child's personal reflection.

Reflection- is an interpretation of what is going on between learning and thinking, the thoughts and opinions that come to mind.

•How do you feel about Alaya throwing milk in Sammie's face?
•What do you think she could have done differently?
•What are your thoughts on Alaya hiding the letter from her mom?
•What do you think about how Alaya's mom explained Chocolate Dirt to her in a positive way?
•Have you had a situation where someone made fun of you or called you a mean name? If so, how did you handle it? After reading Chocolate Dirt, how could you handle the situation in a positive way?
•Why do you think Alaya's mom was crying?
•What are five positive words you can say about yourself?

MIRROR, MIRROR

WHAT DO YOU SEE?

A Reflection of Me.

Having a positive **self-image** is important for any child. Children often believe what their peers/friends say/think about them. This small activity will help your child see the beauty they possess from their own eyes, how they feel and see themselves. Their reflection represents their true self, their inner thoughts/feelings reflect who they really are. **Self-image** is the way you think about and view yourself.

Items needed.
- Small plastic mirror or hand mirror
- Mirror markers
- Sticky notes
- Stickers (pictures, words)

Have your child look in the mirror, then use the above items to decorate their mirror based on the reflection they see. They can use their mirror as a daily reminder of how they see themselves and to feel good in their own skin.

Extended Activity

Hands on activities reinforce what was learned, which further highlight the skills and concepts that were addressed in the story. This activity will inspire children to learn by doing and allow them to take control of their learning through creative and individual explanations of the story.

CHOCOLATE DIRT

DESSERT

Children will enjoy making and eating this delicious, quirky treat.

Ingredients:

Snack Pack Pudding cups

Small bag of gummy worms

Oreo cookies (2-3)

Chocolate chips (optional)

Process:

Children will crumble up Oreo cookies (you can place them in a zip lock bag and use a spoon or fist to break up cookies). Open the pudding cup and place 2-3 gummy worms in the pudding. Sprinkle Oreo cookies and a few chocolate chips on top of pudding. Now place gummy worms on top of the pudding cup, grab a spoon and enjoy the delicious taste of chocolate dirt.

Printed in the United States
by Baker & Taylor Publisher Services